Shots

Nand K Agarwal

First Published in October 2021

ISBN: 978-93-5472-505-0

BLUEROSE PUBLISHERS
www.bluerosepublishers.com
info@bluerosepublishers.com
+91 8882 898 898

Cover Design:
Team Atmoz

Typographic Design:
Team Atmoz

Editor:
Shreya Aggarwal, Nand K Agarwal & Team Atmoz

Distributed by: BlueRose, Amazon, Flipkart

Disclaimer:

This is a work of fiction. An outcome of Author's imagination only. Any resemblance to any person dead or alive is purely co-incidental & un-intentional. Do not try at home. No animal or person was hurt in writing this book!

Acknowledgements:

Nothing that I do is possible without the love & support of people around me. Thank you for giving me the space to dream and imagine!

My Beautiful Wife: Shreya. My Daughter: Neeya & My Son: Shaayan

- My Mother & Father.
- My Mother-in-Law & Father-in-Law.
- My Sister Harsha, BIL- Rohit &nephew Atharv.
- My Friends & Teachers from Hampton Court, Mussoorie.
- My Friends & Teachers from Scindia School, Gwalior.
- My Friends & Teachers from Sukhdev College of Business Studies-New Delhi
- My Friends & Teachers from IIM- Khozhikode
- My work Colleagues
- My Clients
- My Publishing Partners
- Everyone else who has been a part of My journey.

Art & Image Credits: Special artists from Rural India. You will observe that we've used fine traditional Indian art-work in this book. All images are Hand-drawn & optimized digitally.

Digital Design & editing: Team Atmoz

Who is Nand Kishore Agarwal?

Nand is a proud alumnus of Hampton Court- Mussoorie, Scindia School-Gwalior, College of Business Studies-DU& IIM-K. He comes from a small town Muzaffarpur-Bihar but is now settled in the NCR region.

He started his career in the BFSI sector. He is currently the Founder & CEO of Atmoz Industries & Contrarian Ventures LLP. The group has interests in Air Purifiers, Copper Bottles, HR Technology, Actuarial Consulting, Risk Management, Content Creation & a lot more.

Vocationally he loves to teach needy kids & adults, engage with upcoming Entrepreneurs. He loves to travel & explore.

He is an ardent supporter of plastic free, clean & green cities.

Why did he dare to write?

Writing is Nand's 1st love. From being an editor in school to drafting corporate proposals to his 1st Book- its come a long way!

So when initially he thought of becoming a professional writer, that idea was shot down by almost everyone on the 'acknowledgement' list.

"lekhak banoge" 'I will not marry you' 'kharcha kaise chalega' 'future ka kya hoga'

So after fulfilling his responsibilities of 'settling down' & relatively 'establishing' himself he chose to quickly get back to his 1st love. You know how 'pahla pyar' is.

What all does he write?

Nand can write on a variety of subjects. Fiction, non-fiction, management, mythology, research papers, jingles, policies, poems, etc. He can write in English & Hindi both. This book is his 1st attempt & hopefully more will come.

Why isn't Nand talking directly?

Hey Guys! Thank you for picking-up this book. I have enjoyed researching & creating these 8 Shots. All characters are so relatable & take you on a unique journey. I've tried to keep things short & sweet. Please 'bottoms up' in one-go!!

Do write back with all your feedback- good- bad - ugly ☺

We'll try and include some in the next print edition. Also there are exciting gifts to be won (details on the last page)!

Shots: Will certainly excite!

Take risks, the end is the same for everyone!

Chapter Summary:

1. London Dreams:
    a. Total Words- 1309
    b. Main Protagonist: Neha
    c. The story is about Neha's ambitions & how her life changes on a work assignment to London.

2. Locked Down:
    a. Total Words- 1720
    b. Main Protagonist: Meenakshi
    c. The story revolves around physical & emotional distances created because of COVID. Meenakshi- a married woman is able to discover her true feelings.

3. Liberated Soul:
    a. Total Words- 1735
    b. Main Protagonist: Sneha
    c. Sneha is a free soul. She faces her emotional turmoil when she finally falls in love.
4. Lust:
    a. Total Words- 1777
    b. Main Protagonist: Sanjana
    c. Sanjana is mother, wife, middle aged working woman. She tries to bring back the lost spark in her married life.

5. Lost & Found-Love
    a. Total Words- 2199
    b. Main Protagonist: Seema
    c. The story is about Seema's first love gone wrong. How it impacted her & what it took to heal her heart.

6. Limits:
    a. Total Words- 2197
    b. Main Protagonist: Riya
    c. Riya is a young college going girl. Her life is limitless but she has limits too.

7. Love & its Affairs:
    a. Total Words- 3294
    b. Main Protagonist: Gauri
    c. Gauri is a divorcee. She is a successful professional who has learnt to live & enjoy alone. Will love strike her?

8. Love in Silence:
    a. Total Words- 3321
    b. Main Protagonist: Bindu
    c. The story is set in rural India. There are rules, traditions, restrictions, poverty, deprivation & suffering. Can love still find a way?

Index

1st Shot:

London Dreams 2

2nd Shot:

Locked Down 9

3rd Shot:

Liberated Soul 19

4th Shot:

Lust 29

5th Shot:

Lost & Found Love 39

6th Shot:

Limits 51

7th Shot:

Love & its Affairs 63

8th Shot:

Love in Silence 81

1st Shot: London Dreams

1st Shot:

London Dreams

It had been over 3 months now. Work took her to London & he had to stay put in Mumbai.

Neha & Rachit had recently met & started seeing each other. It had been a jolly good one year. They had hit off almost instantly after meeting at a common friend's party. Minor on-off flirting had graduated into a serious affair between the 2. Both were young, into late twenties; educated, aggressive & well sorted in their lives.

Neha was a pretty girl with the magical figures, logical mind & a throbbing heart. She was doing very well in her career. Her job had a very special place in her life & she knew how to call the shots.

This London project of her company was important for her career. She had worked very hard to get it. Today she was really excited. She was finally going to represent her company on this project to London.

Smarty, today the party is on me, screamed Neha into her phone.

Wow wowwow..what is the good news, asked Rachit.

8pm at my place & please carry the wine, requested Neha.

Sure love, Rachit hung up the phone.

The party was a quiet candle lit romantic dinner at Neha's home. She was just perfect with hosting these romantic quickies.

I'm impressed girl, teased Rachit taking Neha into his arms.

She wanted to melt away but she resisted.

The desert may be served only after dinner, Sir. Neha quipped with a wink & escaped.

Over dinner, Neha broke the good news. Rachit's expressions were mixed. He was elated but at the same time was worried & apprehensive. He could manage a broad smile.

That's awesome Neha!

Neha sensing that un-ease, got up & embraced Rachit tight. Rachit reciprocated emotionally.

I'll be back in 4 months love. Time flies, Neha whispered.

Rachit was very happy for her. At the airport they hugged each other, held hands & with a few rolling tears Neha kissed him goodbye. Rachit waved as she dashed to the airport entry gate & disappeared into the crowd.

The initial few weeks in London were hectic for Neha. She had kind off anticipated it only & was prepared. She had to settle down in her small studio apartment, had to get used to her new office, new colleagues & most importantly- her new Boss- Jessica.

Jess was a tuff middle aged Brit woman. She meant business. Results & only results mattered. How you got it was not important. Neha was getting this feeling that she will find it difficult to gel with Jess. Neha was determined; she was not going to let anyone or anything kill her London Dream.

One night, in the solitude of her apartment she was sitting next to the fire place. It was snowing outside. Neha loved snow. She did not get time to sit & appreciate London for its beauty & brilliance. She was staring at her phone. She realized that she had actually not spoken to Rachit. It had been over 15 days. He had called an umpteen number of times & she had hang-up with the one-liners & few consolatory emojis. She picked the phone & dialed. The 2 minutes call had converted into a massive argument. She hung the phone & cried. She missed Rachit that night. Probably for the first time she landed in London. She wanted him. She wanted him right now.

Neha & Jess had a dinner meeting with Fred. They had been chasing him for a while & it was important for them to convince Fred to give the site contract to their company. Fred's contract would ensure that Neha gets a permanent position in the London office. A bigger apartment, that fancy car & the NRI status she always wanted.

Dinner was cordial & everyone got along well. Fred agreed to give Neha & Jess a fair chance. Jess paid the bill & they left the restaurant together. Neha was waiting for her cab.

Can I drop you somewhere? asked Fred from behind the wheels of his white BMW convertible. Fred was in his late forties, had sharp Brit features, owned a company & drove a BMW.

Thank you, that is very kind of you, said Neha.

Fred was driving when Neha's phone rang. Fred was taking Neha to the site for a 3 day visit.

Hi Rachit

Hey Neha-How are you?

Can I call you back Rachit?

There was silence.

Neha thought that once she returned to London after this work trip with Fred she will call Rachit & make up for all the mess between them. She for once realized that she had not been able to give the relationship "time". Time was the vital oxygen for any relationship to survive.

They reached the site after a 3 hour drive. Fred & Neha got along well. Fred loved to boast about his business conquests & his work trips across the world. He even mentioned being to India 3 times. Neha gave him a patient hearing. Fred liked this the most as this was something that most Brits found it difficult to do- listen. May be that's way Fred liked being in Neha's company.

They checked into a Motel. In the next 3 days they had to conclude all the formalities so that the agreements could be signed between both the companies. Jess was to join them shortly. Neha was quick to get on with work. This trip & this project were important for Neha. She hoped to conclude this deal with Fred.

Fred never missed any opportunity to flirt with Neha. He had been making subtle advances. Off lately, the advances had become more frequent & less subtle. Neha politely rejected many but she let a few pass as well.

Neha was used to male attention & could handle things. She had been in similar situations earlier & knew just when to eject. At this moment the only thing on her mind was the project closure. This contract was her golden ticket to London. Fred was important. It was only about a few days.

Today was their last night at the site. Everything had worked out as per the plan. Jess was happy & she congratulated Neha. Neha could finally smell the London dream now.

Fred asked Neha out for dinner that night. She agreed.

Fred was dressed formally. Neha wore her best party outfit.

You pretty damsel, commented Fred as he held Neha by her waist & walked her into the restro-bar. The place was nice, the music soothing, the food good & the wine was awesome. They ate, laughed, and danced. Fred was taking his chances. Neha didn't seem to mind either. At one moment Fred came close to Neha & pulled her in. She could feel his breath & his stiff body. She could hear his heart thump. Her own heart missed a few beats. In a flash they kissed. It was intense. Suddenly, Neha repulsed & nudged. There was noise all around but silence between the two. Neha left & Fred had to follow her out.

Fred dropped Neha to her room & walked away. He was visibly disturbed.

Neha crashed onto the bed & dug her face into the pillow. She thought of Rachit. How would she tell him about this? Her dreamy eyes were wet. She was for once terribly confused. She desperately hoped Fred would not take any offence & that the deal would just sail through as agreed.

Her mind was sprinting in all directions & calculating all possibilities when her door bell rang. It was 2 am in the night. Neha opened the door& saw Fred standing. He was in his night gown & was staring down at her. She looked back at him. Neha took a deep breath, held his hand & let him in.

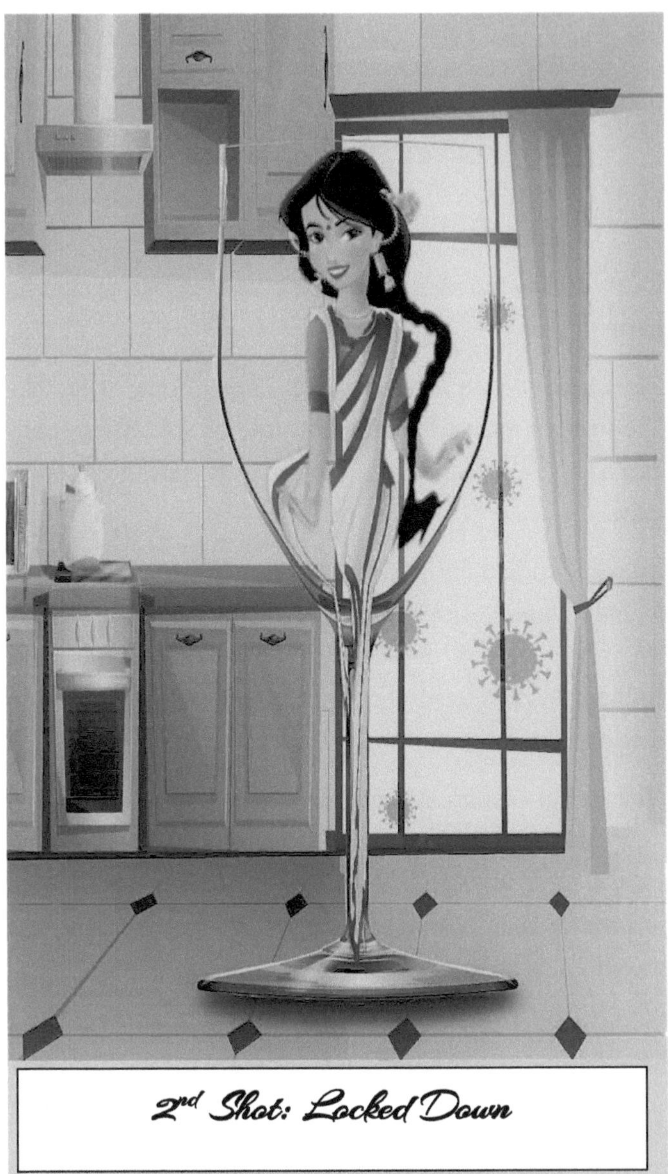

2nd Shot: Locked Down

2nd Shot:

Locked Down

COVID has tested mankind for a lot of things- Including Love.

Meenakshi was a lovely, young, happy house-wife. She had just got married to Sumant. It was Nov 2019. They had a simple arranged marriage & were quick to discover Love.

Sumant worked for a travel company in Mumbai. Life in Mumbai comes with its share of challenges. Sumant's job was very hectic & demanding. To make life ends meet Sumant worked hard. To strike a balance, he made sure that his love nest was always throbbing.

Meenakshi was an amazing cook. One night in between their usual flirtations, Sumant suggested that she should start a tiffin service. It would get them some additional income & keep Meenakshi occupied when Sumant was travelling & busy with work in general.

What if some customers' don't pay for the tiffin? asked Meenakshi.

Someone had to be a fool to choose not to eat food cooked by your lovely hands, quipped Sumant with a wink.

Pamphlets were soon printed & Meenakshi's Kitchen was launched.

Meenakshi had worked hard to prepare a menu, arrange kitchen equipments, delivery tiffins & a lot more. Sumant was helpful & hands-on in the entire process. Meenakshi had thought that business or no business she will not compromise on the quality of her food. Within no time she was supplying tiffins to scores of office goers in her society & nearby.

Meenakshi quiet liked what she was doing. She was simple woman, polite & very friendly. Her approachable nature ensured that everyone in the vicinity got to know her. Her kitchen was becoming famous & so was she. With the new found recognition she did feel like a small celebrity at times. Income streams had also become favorable. She recovered most of her initial investment very soon.

There were periods when Sumant was out-station for days because of work. The kitchen took away Meenakshi's day time but after pack-up, the nights were mostly very lonely. She was not used to being alone & often craved for companionship.

Meenakshi's door bell rang one early morning. She was bathing & was not expecting anyone. Sumant was travelling. She thought it could be the grocery supplier but he was not due to come today. The bell rang again & then again. Meenakshi hurried. She quickly showered, rinsed the soap off her body. She tied her wet hair into a bunch, slipped into her gown & dashed for the door.

Hello Maam! I'm Amit. I've just shifted next door & want to start my tiffin. Meenakshi looked at him sternly & he stared back at her. Water was dripping from her wet hair.

Its 6:30am Amit, said Meenakshi with an obvious display of anger.

Oh sorry Maam, I work in a call-centre & just returned from work.

Amit apologized & turned to leave.

Wait, said Meenakshi. She went in to get her order diary. Amit could not help but appreciate Meena's beauty. Obviously a bit exposed now.

Meenakshi & Amit being neighbors often bumped into each other. Initially Meenakshi ignored him like they've never met. Gradually she started to reciprocate to Amit's Hi & Hellos. Concealed smiles & solitary one-liners were also exchanged at times.

Amit was a young guy. He had also recently shifted to Mumbai. His job kept him away at nights & he was at home in the morning.

Hey Meena, the food was awesome yesterday, Amit shouted from behind.

Meenakshi was returning from the market. She was loaded with vegetable bags.

She turned back & saw Amit coming towards her.

My name is "Meenakshi" & thank you for the feedback.

Can I help with those bags Meena? I'm anyways going up only.

Meenakshi was happy letting go off some of the heavier vegetable bags.

Thank you Amit!

No problem Meena, but can you send biryani tomoro. I just love it.

Meenakshi was a little amazed by his frankness.

We have a fixed menu Amit. You will get what's there in the menu.

Thank you Meena!! The Biryani was the best I've ever had, announced Amit barging into Meenakshi's home.

The door was open & he did not bother to ring the bell or knock. The grocery supplier had just left & Meenakshi had gone to take her shower. She had certainly shut the door but somehow may have missed latching it. Meenakshi's heart missed several beats.

How have you entered the house Amit? Meenakshi asked with anger.

Amit realized that he had made a mistake & immediately apologized.

I'm sorry Meena, the door was open so I just came in to thank you.

He could listen to the water flow from the shower & imagined how Meena would be like- wet. He could see Meenakshi's clothes lying on the bed. He quickly patted his head to get his senses back. He had actually made a mistake & didn't want to offend Meenakshi any further.

Can you please wait outside Amit? shouted Meenakshi from inside the washroom.

She could hear footsteps fade. She took a deep breath & thought what a massive blunder it had been.

Sumant had often joked about Meenakshi being the crush of the society. After all, the way to a man's heart is through his stomach. Sumant pulled Meenakshi into his arms & switched off the lights. Meenakshi melted away. She thought of telling Sumant about Amit. But she was too over-whelmed to discuss anything now. This is exactly what she keeps waiting for. She embraced Sumant tightly & closed her eyes.

It was end of Feb 2020. Sumant was taking a Travel group to Europe. It was his 1st international event & he was so excited. Sumant had toiled hard for this. If this event was a success it would give wings to his career. Sumant had put in all his efforts to ensure that nothing went wrong.

Meenakshi was excited, worried, tensed & a lot of other things. Overall she was happy but she was uncomfortable.

I'll be back in only 15 days.

Only? questioned Meenakshi. How will I manage everything?

You can always ask Amit to help you, joked Sumant. He has been hitting on you off-lately, he teased.

And what if I miss you, asked Meenakshi.

Sumant planted a kiss on her forehead & hugged her tight. Meenakshi embraced him with all her strength. She knew Sumant had to go & as a good wife she must support her husband.

Meenakshi prepared the traditional pooja thali & applied a tilak on Sumant's forehead.

Take care of yourself & call me daily, said Meenakshi holding her tears.

Sumant looked at Meenakshi one last time, picked his bags & left.

Meenakshi watched the taxi go with moist eyes.

Covid had struck & damage across the world was being reported on all television channels. Lock-down was announced. Gradually the entire world was shutting down. Meenakshi was glued to her TV- devastated. Sumant was to return next week. He had called to tell Meenakshi that his flight had been cancelled. He was speaking to his Head Office but was not sure what will happen next. Meenakshi wept the whole night.

She was woken by the sudden loud banging of her door. It was Amit.

What is the matter? she demanded.

The city is closing. We need to stock up on groceries & veggies immediately. I've seen big lines everywhere. You must come with me immediately to get the supplies. He said looking at Meenakshi. He realized, that she was looking pale & her eyes were swollen.

Are you alright Meena? He asked with genuine concern.

Meenakshi burst into tears. Amit held her & helped her take a seat. It was the first time he had touched her. It was the 1st time someone other than Sumant had touched Meenakshi.

Amit came back in the afternoon with sack-full of groceries. He also helped Meenakshi stack things in her kitchen.

Thank you! said Meenakshi.

The lockdown had meant shutdown of Meenakshi's Kitchen. Amit however, continued to take his tiffin from Meenakshi.

Can we have lunch together he asked her one day? I mean I'll continue to fetch groceries for you & you can continue to cook for me. Both of us might just survive, he reasoned.

Ok, said Meenakshi.

In just a matter of a few days, Meenakshi's world had come crashing down. She was alone & helpless. Her Kitchen was shut. A lot of customers had not paid her for the previous month. It was difficult to speak to Sumant.

International calls were expensive & his company had put limits on everything. The only thing to look forward to now was having lunch with Amit.

Lunch had become a regular thing. They chatted & started to discover. They spoke about child-hood, friends, girl-friends.

Do you have any, asked Meenakshi?

Why would you want to know? asked Amit.

Meenakshi was quiet& a little embarrassed. Amit looked at her & smiled.

I had one, but we split before I moved to Mumbai.

Why did you split? Meenakshi wanted to know.

Some-other day, smiled Amit.

Can I ask you something Meena?

No, said Meenakshi, instantly.

That whole night Meenakshi only thought of Amit. She was scared. She was nervous. There was anxiety. Next morning when she stood in the shower she was still thinking about Amit. Water was flowing down her well sculpted body. Thoughts were flowing down her frozen mind. Emotions were flowing down her throbbing heart. Something had happened.

She realized what she was missing in her marriage with Sumant.

Amit did not come for lunch that day. Meenakshi got worried. She thought of calling him to check. She realized she did not have his number on her contact list. She hurriedly searched for her order diary & quickly flipping through the pages she found his name.

Hello Amit, this is Meenakshi. I was waiting for you to come for lunch.

She could hear him cry on the other side. Meenakshi was worried & without wasting anytime she dashed to his apartment.

Amit had lost his father to COVID. He could not even go to his home town to attend the funeral.

Meenakshi sat next to Amit & held him. Amit wrapped his arms around her & wept inconsolably. Meenakshi could feel his tears roll down her neck. She put her arms around him & closed her eyes.

3rd Shot: Liberated Soul

3rd Shot:

Liberated Soul

Love is limitless… countless.. soul-less… ruthless..

Its over Rajat. I can't carry on with this baggage any more. TC- Sneha

Sneha had decided to move on after a 16 month 22 days relationship with Rajat. This was the longest she had 'survived' with a single person in any relationship. She did not believe in giving reasons or explanations for her break-ups. Rajat did not even get the opportunity to absorb the shock. He was cut-off & blocked instantly.

Sneha was a determined, young, promising journo. She was pretty & smart. Always on the move, always exploring, always seeking new adventures. Free bee…liberated soul.

Rajat was the 4th person who became close & personal with Sneha. Sneha had this unique ability to commit to a relationship & put all her heart, mind & body into it. Then she could just pull the plug & shut down things as if nothing has ever happened. Love had no fixed meaning for her. It was fluid. It had to be experienced. It could have different meanings with different people at different times. She was selfish. Well that was Sneha.

Ankur- a new comer (fresher) to the team had just been assigned to Sneha. Since she was a senior & had been in the trade for some time, she had been given the job to train & mentor him. This was not the first time a fresher had been assigned to her. Sneha was notorious with freshers. She had a fixed strategy with all freshers who were assigned to her. In the initial month just grill them, roast them & by chance if they survived, then in the 2nd month raise a 'toast' with them.

Not many were fortunate enough to enjoy a round of drinks with Sneha.

Sneha was already 6 pints down & had ordered for the 7th one. Ankur was nervous. Looking intermittently between his watch & mobile he was just hoping for this 'ordeal' to finish fast. He was on his 1st drink only.

Maam, I think you should not drink now. He uttered after gathering some strength.

Why fattu? Screamed Sneha..can't you handle a drunk girl.

Get us 4 shots she ordered. Ankur was pale.

All yours young boy, she smiled.

Ankur had no choice but to gulp them all down. One-by-one.

He was sloshed.

Sneha dropped Ankur home that night. What a looser she thought.

Ankur got the best passing remarks from Sneha. It was the best remarks for any fresher who had come to Sneha in this company. This had to mean that Ankur was really good at his work. Sneha's positive assessment got Ankur a promising project with the company. He was very excited about it & looking forward to it.

All the best rookie! Be in touch, said Sneha while patting Ankur on his back.

Sure Maam, Thanks a lot! said Ankur

Ankur was 5 years junior to Sneha. Slim, specy, cute, A+ grader, obedient etc. The Marriage Material (TMM) types. Hope he is not a virgin thought Sneha. It had been 4 months now that Sneha had been without a functional boyfriend. It was 5pm & she was still in office wondering what to do.

Why am I thinking about that rookie? she grinned.

Hey Ankur, how are you?

I'm good Maam said Ankur.

Sneha had dialed Ankur. She was not the one to just sit and only think. She was fast with her decisions.

Have you ever dated a woman?

Yes Maam…I mean No Maam, blushed Ankur.

Get ready said Sneha & hung up.

Sneha had decided to get Ankur transferred back to her team. This was not very difficult for her.

Ankur loved to write stories & hence had chosen Journalism. He was shy & spoke only when required. There was a certain mystery about him which probably caught Sneha's fancy. Still waters run deep.

Welcome back buddy. Did you miss me? asked Sneha.

No Maam, I mean Yes Maam...gushed Ankur.

I will take you out for dinner tomoro, she announced. We need to break the ice dear.

Drinks were served. Sneha was looking hot. Her velvet dress just clung to her voluptuous body. Covering enough & revealing enough. She was looking gorgeous.

Ankur had come in business formals. He tried to look his very best for this un-expected event in his life. Not even in his wildest of dreams did he ever imagine dating Sneha. Ankur though never missed the chance to eye scan her. He always thought of Sneha as a hot but rude & strict boss. He could never gather the courage to appreciate her physicality & tell that to her. Who had that courage any-ways. Nearly half the office had a crush on her & the other half would have been females or elderly.

Today, Ankur was out on a dinner date with Sneha. He was counting his blessings. Fingers crossed.

Are you virgin Ankur?

Yes Maam..i mean yes Maam, exclaimed a visibly embarrassed Ankur.

Food was served. Conversations were mostly around work & the next big story. Sneha took every opportunity to scan Ankur. She had to be sure & you bet, she was very satisfied with her new kill. In between bites Sneha looked up at Ankur & caught him staring at her cleave. He put his eyes down immediately. Sneha smiled & winked. Ankur was red.

Please pack the desserts, ordered Sneha. We'll have them at my place.

Ankur was a complete teetotaler. Sneha made him drink, she made him dance, she made him steal, lie, bunk, scream, abuse, smoke, flirt. Also took away his virginity. Essentials of the profession, she thought. Ankur was not complaining either. He quiet liked his new found fame. He could see that 'respect' in everyone's eyes back in office. He didn't mind being Sneha's 'baby boy'. Sneha lost no opportunity to pamper Ankur & made sure that he was always comfortable.

Sneha had to travel for a few days for some urgent work engagement. This would be the first time Sneha would be away from Ankur ever since they started to date.

I'm going to miss you baby she said, hugging Ankur.

I'll miss you too, said Ankur reciprocating her tight hug with all his sincerity.

I plan to take the week off and go for the rafting trip with friends, he said.

Be a bird said Sneha & rode off.

It had been 2 days. Sneha had not been able to speak to Ankur. She had already started to miss him badly. This was certainly not like Sneha. She had mastered the art of being in control of her feelings. Ankur had not responded to her calls either.

What could it be? She was only getting more anxious.

Call me once you read this message- she texted Ankur.

Sneha was not used to a "no-response". She had never been so desperate either in the past.

It was 1 am in the night. Sneha could not sleep. She picked the phone & called Ankur again.

What's the matter Sneha? asked Ankur sounding concerned.

What's the matter with you dammed, screamed Sneha.

Ankur told her that he was up in the hills & there was no network. They had just come down to the foothills. He had seen her messages & had planned to call her in the morning.

Are you OK, asked Ankur again.

Now I'm, said Sneha.

Sneha had a different feeling for Ankur that night. She was missing him, his innocence, his company, his shy eyes, the smell of his body, his touch. She closed her eyes. She was in love.

Sneha & Ankur had moved in together. It was Sneha's idea & Ankur had little say in it. For Ankur this relationship was a ride he had never planned. Sneha was elder to him age & work wise. He was taking each day as it came. He was having fun & enjoying life. Sneha made sure he had no complaints. Even Sneha was having fun. She had never been so content & peaceful in her life earlier. This feeling of bliss was eternal. But she wanted more.

Sneha, you won't believe what happened today. Ankur came running into the kitchen.

I am now going to become an Editor of a leading magazine.

Ankur had applied for the role of an Editor with a leading magazine sometime back. After considerable efforts & multiple rounds of screening he finally got selected. He was happy & super excited.

Sneha was quiet.

Are you not happy Sneha? asked Ankur, not getting any reaction from her.

You never told me about this, you rascal, she smiled.

Sneha gave him a hug. This hug was different.

Ankur had off-lately started to feel something awkward in the relationship. Sneha was not good with hiding feelings.

There was silence on the dinner table. This had never happened in the last 16 months that they had been dating.

The 2 of them had an amazing comradeire. Sneha being the fire & Ankur the ice. They complemented each other & there was never a dull moment. Sneha had put all efforts to ensure Ankur rose in his career & remained close to her.

Ankur had only gained from this relationship in every way. Sneha was not sure.

So now you are going to go away birdie, murmured Sneha.

Ankur looked up & stared into her eyes. What are you not telling me Sneha, he asked.

I think I Love you rookie- she said. Her eyes were wet.

I love you too Sneha, said Ankur but what's the big deal about it.

Will you marry me Ankur & live with me for-ever. Sneha popped the question.

Ankur dropped his fork. He did not know what to say.

He was certainly not ready for marriage at this stage in his career. He was not even sure if he wanted to marry Sneha. That's how she started the relationship. It was a casual fling. Why does she want a commitment now? Was she jealous of his new found role as an independent Editor?

Too many questions erupted in Ankur's mind simultaneously. He did not know what to say. He remained quiet.

Sneha got up & left the dining table.

That night was the loneliest for Sneha. Her tears were limitless. She wept the longest. She thought of the countless hearts she broke for reason or no reason. She realized what being ruthless was.

Sneha knew what Ankur's answer was.

4th Shot: LUST

4th Shot:

Lust

Love needs Lust to last.

Sameer & Sanjana were married for 20 good years. They briefly dated in college & married soon after. Sanjana was the shy types & Sameer was the star of college. As they say, opposites attract. One day Sameer proposed & Sanjana said a yes.

Sameer wanted some time to settle down in his career & Sanjana was also in agreement. The typical family issues in a love marriage & the pressure that it creates on young minds is exceptional. That fear of losing each other made them marry immediately after college. Soon the kids came & it was one happy family.

Sameer's job just consumed the best out of him. The burden of shouldering a family came early upon him. He never complained about it, rather he took it as a challenge & worked hard to ensure that his family enjoyed the modest luxuries of life. They were well settled, their kids went to the best schools, took the best vacations. Over the years they could build up financial assets & were secure about the future.

On the personal front, Sameer & Sanjana were very cordial & respectful of each other. There was enough space in the relationship which allowed pockets of interdependency to bloom & flourish. There was warmth & emotional comfort. However, their love life was not the same as it used to be.

What had begun as fire in the belly for the two had just got limited to rituals now. Love had become a responsibility.

Sanjana was still excited about life though.

She worked for a Private company. She had this unique ability of balancing work-family. She could always take out time for her-self & do the things she loved. She was always willing to explore & innovate. Responsibilities need not mean end to one's personal aspirations.

She tried to speak with Sameer on many occasions but not much seemed to change. Sameer took his life way too seriously. He had taken her for granted & expected her to be the good wife & mother.

Sanjana always appreciated Sameer's contribution towards their family but she also had needs. Inside Sanjana, there was this mental turmoil. It was building up each passing day. She needed a vent.

Sameer, lets plan a trip to Thailand. This time we'll go without kids. Sanjana suggested to Sameer one day.

She had heard a lot of notorious stories about that country & wanted to explore once.

Sameer smiled & agreed.

They landed in Bangkok & checked in to the Hotel. Sanjana had booked a lavish river-front property.

It was a long time since the 2 of them had been on a vacation-alone. Almost close to a decade. She was hoping to re-ignite their relationship. It was their 1st trip to Bangkok. Sanjana had spared no expense. Much to the displeasure of Sameer, she had decided to splurge on this trip.

Sanjana dressed up in her most exotic attire. Her dress hugged her slim frame. She was looking slender.

You are looking damn hot, remarked Sameer. He realized he had not looked at her like that in a long time.

All yours, said Sanjana with a wink.

They entered the club & took a seat in the VIP lounge area. Sanjana had made the bookings.

The evening was beautiful. The dancers were doing their act, people were mingling, the performers kept the tempo up. Sanjana & Sameer were enjoying their drinks.

The whole set-up was something they had never experienced before. Sameer & Sanjana were having a great time. Seeing Sameer relax, Sanjana felt happy. She was in his arms & swaying along with the music beats. Magical!

While Sanjana was drifting away in her magical world, one male performer approached her & requested her to accompany them on the stage. A few other ladies were also invited. In a flash, even before Sameer could react or respond, Sanjana was gone.

Sanjana was right in the middle of the stage surrounded by over a dozen unclad male & female performers. The crowd was cheering, hooting & screaming with all their might.

Sameer wondered what was going to happen. He just hoped Sanjana was not too drunk & safe.

The male dancers held her, tossed her around, caressed her, touched her.

Sanjana was laughing, responding, enjoying the touch & living every moment. There was lust in her eyes. Lightning in her body. She wanted more.

She caught hold of one of the male dancers & embraced him tight. The dancer taking this as a sign of consent embraced her back. His well chiseled muscular male body pressed hard against Sanjana's slim frame. Her hands were exploring him. He lifted her in his arms and kissed her. She reciprocated. The crowd cheered & showered cash.

Sanjana was flying high. Sameer had sunk deep into his chair.

Sameer, this was a fantasy dear. Thank you so much! You are a darling, said Sanjana while on their way back to the hotel.

Sameer was quiet.

You jealous baby, laughed Sanjana & crashed on Sameer's shoulders.

Sanjana was too drunk. In her sloshed state she was murmuring away her fantasies. It felt as if she had wings & was drifting away. A clogged chamber in her soul was pushed open.

Sameer carried her to the room & she fell asleep quickly. Sameer could not.

Sanjana was fresh like a Tulip the next morning. The suffocation inside her had got a release. It felt as if she got a new lease of life. Sanjana had not planned what happened last night. She just went with the flow. She felt so young, so empowered. She had this teenage like blush on her face.

Sameer had not spoken much though.

Are you still burning my love? teased Sanjana with a peck on his cheeks. She put her arms around him,

Sameer did not respond.

It was just a show Sameer, common. I had fun. I seriously wanted this. I was tired of the monotony. She looked up at Sameer.

His eyes were moist.

Oh..Sameer..I'm so sorry..i did not mean to offend you. She hugged him tight & cried. I love you baby, she said.

Sanjana was trying hard to convince Sameer but she did not want to feel guilty about the whole experience. She did not want to regret it.

The very picture of Sanjana in someone else's arms had taken a massive slice out of Sameer's heart. He was jealous, hurt, nervous, broken, shocked. May be he had not been expressive about his feelings off-lately but he really loved her. Their whole journey together flashed before his eyes.

The fact that over a dozen odd guys were all over her & she was reciprocating just did not sink in. He had never seen this side of Sanjana. She was always that shy, dutiful girl. A lot had changed suddenly.

He could not think. He could not comprehend. He was blank.

I'm going back Sanjana, said Sameer over dinner.

But we still have 3 more days Sameer.

You can continue with the trip if you want, said Sameer.

Sanjana was now furious. She screamed & yelled at Sameer.

Sameer it was a strip club that we went to. There were scores of men & women doing all kinds of stuff. We were watching & enjoying. What's the fuss if I had some fun? What's the big deal if I drifted a bit? I did that with you around. I felt safe dear. Please dont make me feel guilty about it.

Sameer was still quiet. He looked away.

Sameer had made her feel bad. Her head was loaded again. She had missed the physical bond with Sameer for over a decade now. She was doing her duty as a wife & a mother; but seeking physical intimacy was no crime.

She was crying. She was sad, upset & angry. Sameer had done practically nothing to re-ignite their dead sex life. Sanjana had taken the initiative. Sameer should have supported her. Atleast he should have behaved like a sport.

The next morning Sanjana woke up very late. She had this severe headache. She looked around the room. Sameer was not anywhere.

She panicked. Sameer could be angry but he could never leave her and go or what if he actually had gone back. Did she hurt him so much? She looked around the room for Sameer's belongings. His wallet, phone, passport were missing.

She was nervous, scared. Her eyes were wet; her heart was lump & her feet numb.

She searched for her phone & dialed Sameer. He did not respond. She called the breakfast desk of the Hotel. Sameer was not there either.

Taking the next flight back to India was the only thing that came to her mind. She quickly rushed to the washroom to shower.

Her mind was not responding. She was married & had kids. What had this trip come to? She was firm to dump her freedom plans & do what was required for her family dutifully. She wanted Sameer back.

Just as she came out of the shower she was startled to see a man standing at the extreme end of her room.

He was looking outside the window. She held her breath for a second & for once was relieved that Sameer was back. Sensing movement that man turned around.

Good Morning Maam- he said with a broad smile. A was well a well built European. Maybe in his late 20's.

This person was not Sameer. Where the hell was Sameer? Who was this man? How did he get in?

Sanjana froze.

She had just stepped out of the shower in her naturals. A towel covered her wet hair. Her beautiful, slim & wet frame was in total display.

That man continued to look at her lustfully & was smiling mischievously.

Sanjana shrieked with all her might.

Suddenly the balcony door opened & Sameer came in running.

Sameer had gone to pick up Joe in the morning. He had stepped into the balcony to complete a work call while Sanjana was bathing.

Sanjana's shriek quickly got him in.

Oh Joe, meet my wife Sanjana. Sanjana this is Joe, he is a professional escort, introduced Sameer.

Sanjana was looking angelic in her naturals. Sameer realized that both the men were ogling at her like adolescents.

Sanjana burst into tears & fell on her knees. Her world had collapsed so many times in the last 90 odd minutes.

Sameer was quick to cover her & lift her up.

Sanjana buried herself into Sameer. I love you, I love you Sameer, she said sobbing. I love you too, replied Sameer.

5th Shot: Lost & Found Love

5th Shot:

Lost & Found Love

It was their alumni meet. They were meeting after 10 years.

Seema & Varun were together in college. They were really together. After college, destiny took them separate ways.

Heyllo! Dr. Varun, How are you? patted Seema on Varun's shoulder.

Hey, Hey Madam! Look at you, responded Varun. Pretty as ever!

You've grown old, young man, teased Seema.

Time flies no Seema. Just some grey hair. Thank you & so good to meet you, said Varun.

Seema & Varun were dating in college. Good 28 months they were together exploring what life had to offer. Seema was a die-hard romantic but Varun was not. Seema was this typical Delhi girl, full of energy, chirpiness, vibrancy, positivity, that zeal to explore life & have fun. She was outgoing, friendly & easily approachable. Seema was beautiful. You could say this basis the number of roses she got on the V-day. Way too many! Guys will have a crush on almost anything female but Seema was special.

Varun was a small town boy. He came to Delhi with eyes full of dreams & hands full of responsibilities. He had to become 'something' in life soon. His father had sacrificed much to be able to send him to a modern college in Delhi. The future of a lot of children in his village was dependent on how Varun fared in his career.

This burden was clearly visible on all his vital organs. He never wasted anytime enjoying life. He was clearly a topper & the most disciplined boy in the class. His only claim to fame!

Seema & Varun: They were not meant for each other- atleast as per rules. Cupid has its own innovative ways to strike. What began as serious exchange of study notes soon graduated to casual exchange of love notes.

It was Seema who proposed & Varun didn't waste any-time in saying a Yes.

Seema was all-in, in this relationship. She was very bullish about Varun. She wanted to marry him & start a life with him. She had this long laundry list of small and big things she had planned to do with Varun.

Varun was too focused on studies. He had many miles to go before he could start dreaming. Seema's presence in Varun's life did make him realize & appreciate the colors of life but her narratives were more of illusions to him.

In this relationship, Seema had invested her heart, mind, soul & body. Varun: only his body- some heart as well.

College was soon going to get over & Seema was getting anxious with each passing day. She wanted Varun to meet her parents. Normal students at this stage are worried about grades & jobs.

Seema's priorities were different. The only thing on her mind was marriage & how quickly it could happen. She was deeply & madly in love. Love's final destination has to be marriage so the sooner you get there the better!

One day after classes Seema invited Varun to meet her parents. Varun had for long avoided this. He did not want to go today as well. Varun for some reason was sure that this meeting would be a disaster. He knew how affluent Seema was & how humble his background was. There was no match, atleast at this moment. Seema resorted to some tried & tested bullying & it worked. Varun agreed to go.

Seema's parents wanted them to get married & settle down in Delhi as soon as tomoro. They were not very comfortable with the idea of their daughter having a love affair. There were multiple issues: caste, status, city, money, power.

They initially tried to persuade Seema out of this but when she was rigid they suggested that this "love" be converted into an "arranged" marriage.

What would people say? They reasoned seriously.

Varun tried to reason with them that he needed more time. He had to complete his studies and take up a job to be able to support Seema.

Reasons don't survive in a typical "baniya" Goyal family household.

Seema's father was clear on his terms of the 'deal'.

Varun & Seema fought like bulls. Things got worse & they refused to talk to each other. No one made any effort to build a bridge. Fissures became gaps, the gaps soon became gulfs.

Varun had secured a scholarship in a top university & flew to the USA for his MBA. Seema didn't even wish him good-bye.

Love is strange. You can love some-one like there is no tomoro & you can also hate that some-one with all your might. How strong can a grudge be? How long can it last? How weak can love be?

After this incident, Seema's father vowed never to let Varun into the house again. Seema's mother orchestrated that perfect heart stroke.

Varun had not called. Seema was not allowed to call. Seema was married off into an affluent 'baniya' family. She moved to Melbourne, Australia.

So, DOCTOR Varun it is, smiled Seema. There was ample sarcasm.

Seema Goyal is now Mrs Seema Dhibrewala, laughed Varun. Wasn't Goyal better?

Verma would've been best, replied Seema. There was silence.

Dr. Varun Verma, after his MBA, went in for his PHD. He had secured the revered & treasured Permanent VISA of USA. He was well settled in NY-New York. He had a steady job & was minting Dollars by the weight. He recently got married (arranged). He had no apparent complaints from life.

Seema had- Too many.

Seema's married life was cordial. She had a healthy relationship with her husband. Her life in Melbourne was sorted. She was very well taken care of. But she always felt a void. Her world was not complete. There was this anger inside her. Shecould never gather the courage to acknowledge it.This anger deep within was slowly burning her down.

She was angry with her parents for the way in which they treated her. She was angry with her-self for allowing all this mess to happen. Above all she was angry with Varun. When she saw Varun's name in the list of participants for the alumni meet, she immediately booked her tickets.

10 years Varun. You didn't bother to make one call.

Varun was quiet.

You could not write one email. My mail id has not changed.

Seema wanted to talk. She had a lot to talk.

Varun was caught off-guard. He had anticipated this confrontation with Seema. But he was not sure how it would spread out.

Varun in general was a sorted guy. He clubbed the Alumni meet dates with his work conference. According to him most problems in life could be broken down into multiple smaller problems & solved- typical MBA. He realized Seema was staring through him. She was waiting for a response.

Can we meet tomoro in Starbucks-CP 4pm? suggested Varun. It may not be a good idea to create a scene here. There are too many people.

Seema picked her stuff & left.

Varun continued with his meet as if nothing had happened. He continued to socialize & had a great time with his friends. He built, re-built a lot of connections. He took every opportunity to flaunt his American VISA status.

To add to the flair, the alumni cell had invited Dr. Varun to address the young students the next day. Varun had his collar & chin up.

While leaving the party, he checked the guest list for Seema's number & saved it.

Seema had lived with a volcano inside her for long. She shouldered the responsibilities of being a good wife, a good daughter, a good daughter-in-law with all her heart. As she lay on her bed, she felt humiliated, dejected-yet again & the reason was Varun.

She was married, Varun was married; even if she fought it out with him what could she achieve. What did she want to achieve? She had risked so much to come to this event- Only to meet Varun.

Seema didn't have answers. She decided to meet Varun at Starbucks tomoro.

Heyllo Seema! Thank god you took out time..exclaimed Varun.

Yes Doc, I always had the time; it's you who never bothered.

The note & tone of things to come was set.

Hot coffee was served.

Well, I'm sorry Seema, started Varun. I was not prepared. I could not come; I mean I could not leave my studies & my career. They were important for me.

And what about me? interjected Seema sharply.

Varun looked up at her. Her eyes were already red. She had a 'bindi' on her fore-head & was dressed in traditional salwar-suit. She was looking beautiful.

Seema you & your parents were hell bent on marriage. I was not ready for it. I wanted to become something. There came a point where this entire marriage pressure just took me down. I wanted to escape. I had to prioritize Seema. I hoped you will understand.

Varun tried to put forth a strong line of reasoning in his defense.

Seema's red eyes were now wet.

One drop of tear from a female eye is enough to devastate walls of logic & destroy every line of reason. Here, Seema's tears just didn't stop.

It was probably the 1st time since he left for USA Varun realized how much Seema loved him. She still did. He had been selfish but he had his reasons. Varun had always missed Seema but even he was too upset with everything to make that call. When he got to know about Seema's marriage he swore never-ever to see her again in his life.

Why did you agree to marry Seema? he asked offering her a tissue.

I didn't agree Varun. I was left with no choice. You just disappeared. You broke all communication. I was so alone. You were not there when I needed you the most. And what did you expect of me-To wait forever? Does this satisfy you Dr Varun?

Varun was quiet. He had nothing to say. Probably it was better to be quiet. It was already 8pm. Seema got up to leave.

I'll have to go Varun.

Can I drive back with you? asked Varun.

The Taxi would have taken 25 minutes to Seema's place.

Not a word was spoken by either of them. Seema kept staring outside the window & Varun kept staring at her. Seema didn't even invite him inside. Not that Varun was too keen to meet his 'could-be' father-in-law either.

Thank you Varun, she finally said while leaving the cab.

Varun took a deep breath and smiled. It was a controlled smile.

As Seema lay on her bed that night, she smiled & blushed. She was happy. Some magic had happened. May be it was just this simple but it had taken so long. She still loved Varun. Varun was still practical but that did not matter anymore. She suddenly had the courage to face her feelings & acknowledge it. A mental block had just come off her. She hugged her pillow tight & fell asleep.

Varun was staying at a Hotel in CP very close to his office. While on his way to work in the morning he dropped a text to Seema to check with her if she wanted to meet again. She had not responded.

Varun had a busy day in office. In between work whenever he got time he was only thinking about Seema. For once he hoped if he could just go-back in time & re-set things.

He was scheduled to go back next week. Seema would also go back to Australia. He did not know what & where things would go. As of now he wanted to be with Seema. He wanted to be in her arms-just like old days.

It was 6pm & Varun was still on his work desk when his phone rang.

Hi Seema, All well? he asked a little worried.

Seema had called to check if he would be keen to meet her at India Gate for an ice-cream. They'd often spent time at India Gate after college during their dating days. That place was special.

Same place, said Varun & packed his stuff & dashed.

I feel so better today Varun. I'm sorry about yesterday. Seema smiled & met Varun 'normally'.

Varun could not believe his ears.

Seema! Are you sure? Is this some kind of a test?

No, said Seema & held his hands.

Seema looked fresh. Over the years she had quiet maintained her-self. Not a strand of grey hair or a line of wrinkle. Varun held her hand tight and just stared at her.

Seema, aware of the physical scrutiny only blushed silently.

They took a long walk on the India Gate circle. Hand-in-hand. They tried the bhelpuri & ice cream. They tried to re-call old secret spots. They spoke about the life missed in the last decade. It was a long catch up on a lot of things.

They say a broken heart can heal by just a touch of honest affection. Seema felt nice with Varun.

Seema I've not felt this good in a long-long time. I feel so relieved, said Varun.

Seema looked at him & smiled. Me too!

6th Shot: Limits

6th Shot:

Limits

A happy heart is a treasure trove. An upset heart is a Devil's abode.

Riya was currently dating Rahul. She had just wrapped up dating Mukul; she was just good friends with Abhishek, Romit, Neil & Himanshu. Binny had proposed to her & was patiently waiting for Riya to respond.

Riya could effortlessly glide through relationships like a hot knife through butter.

Obviously she was hot & she was aware of it. Have it flaunt it. She was not the one who would go slow on life. For her, life had no speed breakers. She was confident, she was bright, she was independent & she was in total charge of her life. She loved it.

Riya was in her final semester in college now. She always felt that something was slipping away too fast from her. She wanted to live this moment as much as she could. Somewhere she knew life would change after college.

Riya for sure had her share of college fun. She was one wild party beast. She was the light & sound (read 'siren') of every college party. The perfect party animal (read 'devil').

How much is too much was the question? Riya was still discovering.

Riya was efficient in managing her relationships with the opposite sex. She enjoyed cordial relationships with all her ex BFs & BF-in-waiting.

She was very close to Mukul while they were dating. They had explored every nook & corner of each other's body & mind. Riya-Mukul were well known love-birds. When Riya decided to move on from their relationship they parted ways amicably like matured people.

Riya had fallen for Rahul. Rahul was Mukul's friend. A few casual interactions became a serious affair between them.

Mukul however, was cordial & cool about Riya's relationship with Rahul. Infact, they continued to hang out together as a gang.

Rahul was this uber cool, rich, spoilt guy. Had little to do with studies or anything constructive. He came to college to only hang around & have fun. Rahul hosted some of the best parties in college. He was popular. Riya & Rahul were an item together. Riya had perfect control on Rahul & she made sure she got all that she wanted.

Rahul also splurged on his new fond love without worrying much. Riya was having fun exploring life with

Rahul. Rahul was having fun flaunting his new trophy Girl Friend.

Happy Birthday sweetheart- Riya hugged & kissed Rahul as she gave him a bouquet of red roses.

It was Rahul's B Day. Riya had planned a short fun trip with a select gang of friends to Shimla.

Mukul, Abhishek, Romit, Neil & Himanshu, Binny & a few other guys & girls were invited. A small close-knit group.

Riya had tried to keep this trip a surprise but Rahul got to know of it almost as soon as she discussed the plan with Mukul.

Rahul hugged Riya back as tightly as he could.

Oh dear, this is awesome, he said.

Rahul had been eagerly looking forward to this trip. He was very excited.

This will be my most special birthday; he had mentioned it to his 'boy'gang.

It was near impossible for Rahul to be humble.

The group reached Shimla & checked-in. The Hotel was a comfortable 4 star property on the outskirts of the town. Obviously the expenses were on Rahul. After all it was his birthday party.

All were excited about this fun trip. For many it would probably be the last trip together as a college gang. This being the last semester, college would soon come to an end. They would bid goodbyes & go running after life independently. There were elements of nostalgia.

Riya had personally planned & supervised the whole event. The cake, the drinks, snacks, food, décor, music etc. She was very particular. Things had to be perfect.

The party was planned in the Hotel pub, which of-course was exclusively booked for the 'gang'.

The most difficult part for Riya was to decide on her dress for the evening party. After much deliberation she decided on a 'jucci' mini dress. She looked like a flawless goddess in it.

Riya, how many are you going to kill today, asked Rahul.

I'll begin with you dear, laughed back Riya.

It was evening & everyone had assembled in the party hall as per the plan. They were waiting for the Bday boy & his GF to come. Some VIP treatment ought to be given to the special couple.

Rahul & Riya entered the party hall amongst loud cheer & hoot from their gang of friends. Riya looked like a diva on the hunt. She was aware of the male eyes on her & she loved every bit of the attention that came her way. Rahul held her tight by the waist as they entered the party hall.

The cake was soon cut. Riya smeared the chocolate cream all over Rahul & poured a bottle of Wine over him.

Rahul was creamed & wet. Riya then caught hold of him and hugged him tight- Cheers to The Birthday Boy!

The public was fair to applaud the antic.

Riya was capable of doing anything. She alone could take any party notches up. This was her party. She had to set some standards for posterity to remember. Riya could not disappoint.

Drinks were flowing freely & music played on non-stop. People were dancing, mingling & chatting away to glory. Rahul & Riya were un-separable. It sure was a fun filled evening.

Suddenly, Riya climbed up to the bar table with a bottle of Vodka in her hands. She was sufficiently drunk & was swaying with the music. Her mini dress could do little to conceal the view people got from below.

Rahul & Mukul too got onto the table soon enough. The three of them danced & stomped their feet in sync.

What a sight it was for the gang. Total value for money riot!

Riya got this feeling of a 'Celebrity' in such parties. She was well aware of the eyes scanning her & the intentions of those gazing eyes.

If music was loud & Riya was on fire-feast on!! Riya gave a damn & relished the limelight that fell on her.

Soon enough Riya was sandwiched between these 2 boys. She could feel Mukul press against her back. Rahul pushed hard from the front.

Riya was not unknown to these 2 men or what they had to offer, but this act felt a bit weird. Anyways, she thought. This was not the time to calculate. She just gave into the moment & continued with the fun.

Passions were flying high. Riya hugged Rahul & kissed him. Rahul lifted Riya up into his arms. His hands lifted her dress to reveal much. Her lone red inner had a lot of cover up to do now.

Strip, strip, strip was the hoot that was now coming from the crowd. It got louder & louder. Rahul took off his cream smeared T-shirt & swung it on the crowd below like a 'rock-star'. How could Mukul lag behind? He too took off & flung his shirt.

Now all eyes were on Riya. She looked at the 2 top-less boys & gave that wicked smile.

Not your lucky day, boys!!

Riya just showed them the finger & jumped off.

Things did get pretty intense, thought Riya. The boys below got much more than what they had signed up for. Lucky them, she gushed.

Rahul can lose it at times & today being his Bday he had this 'license' to go wild.

Just got off on time, she thought to herself.

Riya left the party to change. The GF of the Bday boy & the hostess of the party could do good with atleast 2 dresses for the evening. Plus her current dress was smeared with cream & wet with wine.

She quickly cleaned herself & came back in about 15minutes. Reasonably fast for a girl. She felt fresh again.

Her red silk gown revealed the contours of her sexy figure. She looked simmering hot.

Riya! sexy dress, but no inners? murmured Mukul into Riya's ears.

Riya was used to Mukul's one liners but she obviously did not want to explain to him what & how a nip-tape & thong worked like.

Shut up Mukul, she said & walked away.

She was looking for Rahul. She luckily finally found him in a sober, dressed up state.

Thank-God you are in your senses, she sighed.

Riya held Rahul's hand & hit the dance floor. They dancedwith their friends as if there is no tomoro. The DJ was kind enough to oblige to their requests.

Riya realized that Rahul still had some cream on his neck & ears.

Can I lick the cream off, asked Riya?

No! said Rahul.

Riya bit his ears.

You rascal!

The sun was long gone & the moon was high up in the clear skies of Shimla. It was already very late.

Riya was reaching out to everyone as a diligent host to check if they had dinner or not. People were eating their food & leaving. The crowd was thinning out.

What a hectic day, sighed Riya. Hope you had a memorable day Rahul.

Rahul smiled.

Riya, you didn't give me my Bday gift-complained Rahul with a wink.

Riya had organized this special trip, bought roses, bottles of perfume, his favorite watch, had hugged & kissed him, smooched him, danced with him & his friends, was with him while scores of eager eyeballs waited for her attention patiently & this bugger was still complaining. Funny she thought.

What does the Bday boy want now? asked Riya.

Rahul came close & whispered something into her ears. It was a long whisper.

I'll be waiting sexy, said Rahul softly & left for his room.

Riya watched Rahul go. She briefly felt the cold wind penetrate her thin gown & chill her soul. The baby hair on her plunging neckline were now hard. She was numb.

Her body felt nothing. She wanted to think but her mind felt heavy, she wanted to calculate but she could not. It was probably the first time she felt like this.

She had always gone with the flow all her life. She lived it on her terms. She had no regrets. Nobody had ever 'commanded' her to do any-thing. Nobody had ever objectified her.

Rahul had asked her for a threesome with Mukul that night. He had 'discussed' the whole plan with Mukul. He & Mukul were waiting for Riya to come into their room & 'oblige'.

Physical intimacy was not such a big deal for Riya. She was confident about her body & she knew what she wanted from people around her.

There were 'limits'. The fact that Rahul could 'plan' of something like this with the 'boys' & expect her to comply made her feel really bad.

Riya & Rahul spoke about everything. Why couldn't Rahul discuss such a 'fantasy' with her prior to making it public? He had judged her; he had formed an opinion about her. He looked at her through a certain prism that was derogatory. He had taken her for granted.

This thought made her very uncomfortable. It portrayed her in a way that made her feel like a slut. She was angry.

Yes it was Rahul's special day& Riya wanted to make it memorable for him but he just crossed his 'limits'.

She could flirt, she could dress up in a certain way, she could drink, dance, but what gave Rahul the gumption to 'plan' this with Mukul & tell her to do it.

Riya was now furious.

In my room in 30 mins, take a bath & don't knock when you come. Riya sent a text message to Rahul.

Rahul quickly replied back with multiple heart emojis.

Rahul & Mukul's excitement was at its peak. They were soon going to live their wildest fantasy. Both the boys had been physically close to Riya but this was going to be something else.

They cleaned themselves & dressed up. They stealthily came creeping to Riya's room. They had to be sure to avoid suspicious eyeballs.

Riya's room was in the corner, one floor below their room. They quietly pushed the door ajar a little bit. The room was dimly lit. Not too bright & not too dark either.

Oh my god, exclaimed Rahul.

They were surprised to see Riya in her night wear. A black backless sheer gown. Riya was looking hot.

She had her back towards the door & was swaying to some good English music. Every movement of her body made Rahul & Mukul's heart skip several beats. They could not believe their good luck.

Just as they were about to enter her room they saw Binny emerge from the washroom.

Rahul & Mukul were startled.

Binny went and held Riya by her waist. He hesitantly gave her a peck on her neck. She turned around & hugged him before climbing onto her bed.

Can you switch off the lights Binny? & do check the door, she said.

Binny was only happy to oblige!

7th Shot: Love & It's Affairs

7th Shot:

Love & it's Affairs

Never say Never.

Akshay, I've had multiple affairs.

Gauri initiated the conversation- as blunt as her 'blunt' hair cut. It's only fair to be honest at the very outset. This just may not work out between us.

Tea was served by the waiter.

Much to her dis-like she was on a 'matrimonial date' with Akshay. It was arranged by their respective parents.

Gauri had deciphered this strategy to quickly get rid of such ordeals. Initially she used to refuse going on such 'dates'. But parents find ways into bullying their children to listen to them.

Gauri was a 41 year old 'child'.

Gauri was a divorcee & Akshay was a widower. Both were in their forties. It was anyways tough to even evaluate re-starting a life with a new partner at this stage & Guari's approach made it only impossible.

It was obviously not a typical 'matrimonial alliance'.

We can discuss your affairs once we click Gauri. If & once we click your 'affairs' won't matter, replied Akshay with a smile.

Gauri was impressed. She liked the answer. Very unlike Gauri, she smiled back & sipped her tea.

Gauri was your shy, obedient, dutiful girl in college. Good in studies, helpful & talkative.

She had these normal dreams, normal expectations from life. She was looking forward to her life just like every other girl does.

She fell in love with a charming guy. They dated for some time & with the support & blessings of their family they got married. Gauri was excited & ecstatic. Life seemed perfect & promising for Gauri- atleast till this point in time.

They say that marriages are made in heaven. May be this is completely true or may be its just a myth. For Gauri her married life became a living hell almost as soon as she got back from her honeymoon.

Life is different when you are dating. True colors emerge only when you actually spend a life together.

Gauri soon realized that she had made a monumental judgment error with respect to the life partner she chose. It was however too late. She could never imagine life would come topsy-turvy so fast. Her beautiful magical world that she had long dreamt off would actually become a living nightmare.

Monetary demands were made, questions on Gauri's character & up-bringing were raised, her parents were insulted for every little thing.

Initially, Gauri played it down but soon enough she started to protest. Verbal arguments became ugly spats, spats became frequent fights, and fights became a perpetual mental trauma.

One day in between arguments Gauri was slapped by her husband. She hit him back with all her might. Blows were exchanged & Gauri being the 'weaker' sex had to be hospitalized.

Her broken jaw took 2 months to heal but her soul was wounded for-ever.

Police cases, multiple rounds of courts, taunts of the world, loss of job, acute depression came in abundance as a package for Gauri.

These 2 years of torture & trauma transformed Gauri. That shy, dutiful girl all of sudden became as strong as a rock. She stood her ground & fought. She finally won the court case. Her in-laws & her husband were jailed for domestic violence.

Gauri was finally free. She was divorced.

She took a vow: I will never fall in love again. I will never ever re-marry.

It took a close to a decade for Gauri to heal & resurrect her life. Her parents supported her un-conditionally.

After a lot of turmoil, hard work & mental anguish, today she was able to establish herself as an independent & successful professional. She took care of her-self & her parents. She supported all their financials & made sure they lived a good life.

Gauri lost the extra weight that came with depression. She had become regular with exercise & fitness. She got her glow back. She had dumped that baggage of past. Time heals.

Gauri was 'tip-top' in every way of the word. Ready to rule the world. Roaring loud like a tigress.

Gauri was averse to relationships. She was scared to commit. Being pretty & well settled she got a lot of male attention. She wanted a companion, but nothing more than that. She had long dumped the 'soul mate' theory.

She was rich, gorgeous, independent & fearless. She had over the years learnt to fish! Technology had only made things easier. Gauri was now your regular hunter.

Room number 211, Tinger hotel & don't be late. Gauri was giving instructions to someone on the phone.

It was a 'treat' Saturday. The last Saturday of every month was Gauri's wild Saturday night. Gauri had checked in, completed the rituals- bath, hair, hygiene, protection. She was waiting for her 'guy' to come.

The room bell rang. Gauri looked in through the 'peep' hole to re-confirm. She opened the door partially. Gauri re-validated his credentials & then let him in.

Gauri had a wild, ravishing & refreshing session.

She had become a control freak & it quiet reflected in her adventures as well. Gauri liked to be in control. The session had to flow in a certain manner.

The 'guy' was more than happy to oblige.

Gauri instructed him to strip. She played the music & 'guy' soon got into the act.

Gauri took off her clothes & lay on the bed.

She commanded him to give her a massage.

The 'guy' quickly took out the body cream from his bag & proceeded to please her tensed muscles.

Gauri closed her eyes & drowned in the moment.

Lift me and take me to the shower, her voice was gentler now.

The 'guy' wrapped Gauri into his strong arms & took her to the washroom.

Gauri had the cake, the icing & everything that came with it.

These 'guys' were cult professionals & they just know how to satisfy their clients. Specially, the demanding ones!

Gauri approached these sessions with a certain sense of vengeance. She was rude, physically rough & unstoppable. Somewhere her bruised soul was still healing.

But today, Gauri was more than happy. Her batteries were charged, her ego satisfied & her muscles were raring to go again.

Bring it on!

Gauri never bothered about names & as a rule did not meet the same guy twice. She never went back to the same Hotel again. She did not allow the guy to spend the night with her. Just finish the job and leave. As a lone hunter she had her rules. She had to be careful with her moves.

She paid him & even tipped him well. She politely thanked him & asked him to leave.

Gauri had a good time at Tinger. The session was still playing on in her head.

She was at the check-out counter paying the bills at the reception when she heard her name being called out.

Gauri, hey Gauri….

Gauri turned around & looked back. It was Akshay.

Oh…Hi Akshay, how are you?

I'm good, said Akshay.

How are you & what brings you to Tinger? asked Akshay.

Gauri did not reply.

Gauri did not want to get dragged into a conversation at this time. She suddenly had this teenage like blush on her face. She only wanted to disappear from there.

She ignored Akshay & hurriedly paid her bills. She picked her bags & started to leave.

Ok, let me help you with the bags, interjected Akshay.

I insist, he repeated.

Akshay lifted her bags & walked her to the taxi area.

I'm here for a work conference today, he said making an attempt to strike a conversation again.

Oh great, said Gauri, you must get on with it.

Can we go for a coffee or something? I mean anytime suitable to you.

Akshay proposed again, trying desperately hard to get something out of Gauri.

Ya sure, said Gauri.

Give me a call & we'll fix up. She said while entering her taxi.

She didn't even realize to thank him for helping her with the bags.

She could see him wave good-bye. Thank- god, what an escape, she smiled. Gauri had no plans to meet Akshay again.

Gauri had to leave for a scheduled week long business trip. She finally completed her packing.

Restricting your clothes to the Air line weight limit was just criminal. She was of the opinion that girls must be allowed to carry as much luggage as they wanted. Men should be given limits.

She was giving her parents those last minute instructions. Food, ration, grocery, medicines, laundry, maid, cash , security & a lot more.

Bete, what have you decided about Akshay. He is a good boy. Gauri's mother was trying her luck again.

We'll talk about it when I'm back from the trip, replied Gauri.

Akshay's Mother had called to say that the 2 of you met last week, pointed Gauri's father.

We didn't meet Dad, we bumped into each other.

It's the same thing Gauri. Why didn't you tell us about it? See, Akshay told his mother about it. Gauri's Dad had a point to make.

Dad, I'm over forty now, can you treat me like one please.

Have a nice trip dear.

I Love you.

Love you too.

She hugged her parents & left.

"We did not meet last week Akshay, we bumped onto each other by accident." She texted Akshay as soon as she got into her cab.

Gauri thought it was better to have it clarified.

It was already 8pm & she was as usual late. She was desperately hoping that the traffic would spare her today. She didn't want to miss the flight. Her boss would be very angry. While Gauri was lost in her panic world, her phone rang.

It was Akshay.

Hey Gauri, what's up.

All good, replied Gauri.

Before, Gauri could complain further, Akshay agreed that they did not meet & that's exactly how he had put it to his mother. She could have unknowingly or knowingly twisted the facts.

I'm sorry if it caused you a problem, reasoned Akshay.

No, no, not at all. You know how parents react when they get to know of such things.

So, are you a late night person Akshay? asked Gauri.

Not really, but it depends on the motivation to be up, replied Akshay.

Why are you up today, asked Gauri.

Well, I look forward to talking to you, replied Akshay. And why is Gauri Madam up to-night?

I've a flight to catch Sir, pointed Gauri.

I lifted your bags for you Madam, just incase you've forgotten. Our coffee is due Gauri.

Do you mind finding some time tonight? Requested Akshay.

I'm flying to Mumbai in the next 2 hours. But you are welcome to meet me at the airport for a coffee, replied Gauri.

After hanging up, Gauri paused for a while & thought. She then smiled & let it go. Akshay was not going to come to the airport by any chance.

Gauri was in the boarding check-in line when she heard her name being called out. The voice was familiar. She turned around and to her surprise it was Akshay.

How, what, why?? Gauri had too many questions.

They dropped their baggage & hit the coffee bar.

You are stalking me Akshay. Gauri complained.

Akshay, could not control his laughter.

I wouldn't mind stalking you Madam but I was booked on this flight 15 days ago.

Are you stalking me Madam, anyhow?

You wish, smiled Gauri.

Coffee was served. Gauri & Akshay could not stop talking. Their conversations continued onto the flight.

Gauri had not spoken so much to anyone in a long-long time. Akshay was fun. She was beginning to like him.

At the Mumbai Airport they bid each other good-bye with a promise to meet up again while they were still in Mumbai. They exchanged their hotel locations.

Akshay was the CEO of his company. His ways were so humble that you could mistake him for a normal office executive. He was simple, knowledgeable & respectful towards all. He had worked up the ladder in his career with honesty & hard work. He lost his wife to cancer some years back.

Gauri had this sudden respect for him.

2 days had passed & neither of them could take out time to call each other. Gauri did think of texting him a few times but she didn't. She had to be careful with her feelings.

It was already evening & Gauri was done for the day. Her Boss had asked her out for dinner. She was in no mood to oblige & was figuring out how to politely decline & chicken out.

She was hoping Akshay would call & they could meet. In between this dilemma, Gauri's boss asked her again for dinner & she finally had to say a yes.

Dinner with the boss was boring as expected. Gauri tried hard not to make her suffering look evident. Gauri was aware of the 'hits' his boss kept trying on her. Nothing was explicit or over-board. Knowing Gauri was single he just hoped to get lucky some day. Over the years Gauri had learnt how to manage him well.

Gauri took a cab back to her hotel. It was late but Mumbai is safe for women. Gauri thanked her driver & dashed to the reception to pick her room keys. She just wanted to crash.

She was surprised to see a huge bouquet in her name. It also had a small note.

I'm bunking office tomoro. Will pick you up at 10am. See you, Akshay.

Gauri was amused. She was blushing & smiling at the same time. What a cute idiot, she thought.

What will she tell her Boss? What will Akshay think if she went out with him? She quiet liked him but was skeptical. What if Akshay proposed? She did not want to get into this emotional whirlwind again. Her mind was working hard as usual.

She dropped her Boss a text that she will be on leave tomoro. She picked the phone & called Akshay.

Gauri: Thank you for the flowers, Mr. CEO.

Akshay: You're welcome Madam, hope you liked them.

Gauri: Very much. They are beautiful.

Akshay: So hope you're coming out with me tomoro.

Gauri: Yes, I guess I'll have to come.

Akshay: So can we call it our 1st official date.

Gauri: You call it whatever you want to call it, idiot.

Good night!

Gauri kept thinking about Akshay the whole night.

She was excited but her turbulent past was holding her back. There was this fear of failure. That fear of trusting someone & getting betrayed again. She had lived with the pain & scars of a troubled relationship for a very long time. She was scared of getting hurt gain.

When Gauri got up she had this smile on her face. It felt weird. She was blushing as if she was going out on her 1st date.

Gauri quickly got on with her beauty rituals. She didn't want to look overly excited but neither did she want to come across as a barrier. Gauri had decided to meet Akshay with an open mind & then leave things to destiny.

She was not sure what to wear. The most common problem with Girls. She finally dressed up in her casuals- Jeans & T-shirt. She did not want to give away too much. Slow & steady was the strategy.

She was ready on time & was waiting for Akshay to come.

Her room intercom rang & she was informed about the arrival of a guest. She was not sure whether to call him to her room or go straight down.

Please ask him to wait at the reception, she politely instructed.

Gauri checked herself one last time in the mirror to re-validate the make-up. She picked her bag & left.

Akshay was standing at the reception desk, neatly dressed in smart casuals. He was looking nice. Gauri waved at him from a distance & smiled. He waved back. Gauri felt like going on a picnic with school friends.

Silly she thought. What kind of teenage stuff was this?

They spent the day discovering Mumbai & discovering each other.

With every minute that they spent together, Gauri's trust in Akshay only increased. Akshay spoke about all his life. He was brutally honest about things.

Gauri was listening patiently.

So Madam, am I the only one who is supposed to talk today? joked Akshay.

Yes Mr. CEO. For now please carry on, I'm enjoying listening to you, replied Gauri.

The beach though dirty didn't feel dirty. The air though moist didn't feel humid. The noise of the vendors didn't feel disturbing. The whole situation was just so peaceful. Gauri had not had such a splendid time in ages.

The sun was already setting in & the wind had become cooler.

Gauri was engrossed in Akshay's stories. The whole day had passed & it seemed as if they had just met.

Akshay had booked the dinner at a plush beachside hotel.

Akshay are you mad, am I going to get into that Hotel like this? Gauri screamed.

But you look beautiful Gauri, reacted Akshay. I mean there is nothing wrong with this dress. He tried to cover up for his 'stray' comment.

A Jeans & a Top can't be a dress dear but thank you for the compliment, smiled Gauri.

There was a moment of awkwardness. It was the first time Akshay had commented on Gauri's physicality.

Over the years Gauri had become so used to the male gaze. She could feel that 'vulturism' in someone's eyes from a distance.

During the whole day with Akshay, he had not once stared at Gauri or said anything loose or lacking in character. Infact he had never done it in any of their past meetings or conversations.

The dinner set-up was beautiful.

Candle lit corner table with full sea view. A private butler & music of choice only added to the luxury.

Amazing place Akshay. I'm impressed, said Gauri as they took their seats.

I'm glad you liked it, smiled Akshay.

They had just settled down. It had been a long day. Both of them were tired.

I'll be back in a while. Gauri excused her-self. She picked her bag & left.

She returned in about 30 minutes. She had changed into a beautiful purple silk evening gown.

She was looking angelic.

Excuse me Madam. Who are you?

My name is Gauri, she smiled back.

Oh Wow! exclaimed Akshay. You carried this dress with you. What was the plan?

To kill, laughed Gauri.

Over dinner, Gauri opened up about her life & how things had been for her.

She was slow to open up but once she started she did not know where to stop.

Akshay was listening with all seriousness & concern.

Gauri suddenly started to cry. Over the years she had learnt how to hide her feelings. She was a strong lady. But even the strongest walls fail to hold tsunamis of such magnitude.

Gauri let her guard down & allowed her emotions to flow free.

Akshay held Gauri's hand & looked her in the eyes.

Life is not always fair Gauri, but it moves on like a river.

I want to make you feel special again.

I want to see you smile always.

I want you to start believing in love again.

Akshay bent on his knees. He was still holding Gauri's hands.

So Maam, will you want to consider spending the rest of your life with me? Akshay was holding a ring.

Gauri was too awed with everything. She dug her face into her palms.

Madam, my knees will appreciate a quick response.

Gauri got up & lifted Akshay. She threw herself into his arms.

Yes, you idiot!

8th Shot: Love in Silence

8th Shot:

Love in Silence

Even Silence has a voice.

Bindu was bathing in the village pond. She was there along with her friends to complete her morning rituals.

She was just 18 years but was way smarter than most of the kids in the village.

Bindu rigorously rubbed the heavily tanned skin covering her slim body with soap. Fairness was a desirable but an impossible task to achieve. A flimsy cotton sheet barely managed to cover her modesty as she lifted its folds in turns to clean her-self- uncovering some part of her body & then covering some. This process did give away a lot to any greedy on-looker.

Times were not cordial & there was a high risk of a miscreant hiding in the trees or bushes.

The girls took all precautions possible. They left early in the morning, never unclothed completely & one girl always stood with a stick as a guard.

The girl on guard duty today was Munni. She was Bindu's best friend. Munni was very possessive & protective about her. There were no secrets between them. Munni always kept an eye on Bindu when she was in the pond.

In comparison to Bindu, Munni was relatively well built & fair. They even went to school together, played together & had virtually grown up together. The villagers called them an in-separable bundle.

Attentive & alert Munni saw a sudden movement from behind one of the bushes.

She quickly blew the whistle. The whistle was a sign of danger & it alerted the girls in the pond. All the girls in the pond quickly got into action. They dressed up in a fraction of a second & hurried to join Munni.

Munni dashed toward the bushes yelling & banging her stick. In some distance she saw 2 boys running away.

By this time Bindu had caught up with Munni. She had picked up a fallen tree branch & was shouting at the un-identified boys along with Munni.

Bachchgaye, sighed Bindu.

It was because of your alertness Munni that we were saved from this massive embarrassment today, exclaimed Bindu.

Munni was still red with anger. Till how long will this non-sense go on? We have to put an end to this, she screamed.

Yes we must put an end to this, but how? Bindu questioned.

Could you recognize anyone? Were they from our own village?

Yes, said Munni. One of them was Virju- the son of the village Panch. We must teach him a lesson now.

Bindu knew that they could do nothing with Virju. It was better to forget & move on.

Yes we surely will, said Bindu comforting Munni & herself.

Bindu held Munni's hand & they went back to the cool & clear water of the pond. They spent some time playing & laughing together. Bindu scrubbed Munni's back & gave her a good head massage.

The massage helped Munni cool down.

Look at yourself. You have become a full grown woman Munni, teased Bindu.

Shut up. Munni was embarrassed.

Bindu's life was tuff, similar to most children in her village. There weren't too many things to look forward to in the village.

People were poor & their thoughts were still regressive. Being a girl only made matters worse.

Going to her school, dips in the pond & chilling out with Munni in the paddy fields were few of the luxuries that Bindu afforded.

She enjoyed these moments thoroughly.

Bindu's father was a gardener at the village Gram Panchayat office. Her mother helped a few wealthy families in the village with cattle cleaning & general household work.

She had 4 more siblings- All sisters. She was the eldest. Her day started early & continued way till the night was dark. Her parents worked hard to ensure that the family never slept hungry & could lead a life of dignity.

Dignity- what was it? Bindu always asked her parents.

Her parents were mostly silent.

She often compared their life with the life of the wealthy kids in the village. Her parents mostly had teary eyes to these questions.

Bindu was those few girls in the village who had dared to dream. She had fought with her family to let her study. It took her a while to convince them. She was now in 12th grade- her final year in school.

Bindu was determined to get a better life; a life of dignity- how? she did not know.

Bindu had decided to go to the town & enroll for college after school. She had keen interest in Arts & wanted to become a Teacher.

Her dreams were modest but her family was hell bent to marry her off as soon as she was done with her school. Bindu was hell bent not to marry- At any cost.

Bindu was made to dress up in her best attire.

A table was also arranged in their hut. 3 types of biscuits, black cold drink & tea were also arranged.

This was a rarity for her family. "Someone' was coming to see her today. Her father had arranged a matrimonial relationship with a modest wealthy family from a neighboring village. The gram panch had to personally put in a word. Bindu was furious but she had to eventually succumb to the pressure of her parents.

The vanity program ended after causing much embarrassment & fury to Bindu. She did not speak to anyone that night.

She silently picked her bags and left for school in the morning.

She had just come back from school. Her head was heavy. Munni had also not come to school today. Speaking to her would have certainly helped.

You are soon going to be a beautiful bride, announced Bindu's mother. She quickly took her bag & offered her a glass of water.

The marriage proposal has been accepted by them. Gleamed Bindu's father.

I'm not going to marry, screamed Bindu. She repeated this again & again.

Tears rolled down her cheeks. Her parents could empathize but could do little for her. They had 3 more kids & life's fuel was limited.

Bindu threw the glass of water & ran away from her hut.

It was scorching hot in the afternoon. Bindu was angry & afraid. She knew her choices were limited. Sitting under the shade of a huge Banyan tree near the pond she was contemplating her options. Her eyes were wet. Her vision was blurred.

She thought of meeting Munni. At this time of the day Munni would be at the village Hospital. She worked there as a helper after school & made some good money. Bindu got up & started to walk towards the Hospital.

Munni's social status was similar to Bindu's. But somehow Munni always found ways to earn money. She was very enterprising. On many occasions Munni had given money to Bindu as well. Of course Bindu had thought of returning it as and when she got a job.

Bindu reached the hospital & asked the helper bhaiya if he had seen Munni. He pointed upwards towards the patient wards on the 1st Floor.

Normally, the hospital is mostly vacant. It had one doctor & one nurse as full time employees. Illness in village was mostly seasonal. Since this was peak summers the load on the hospital was minimal.

Bindu reached the operation theatre on the 1st floor searching for Munni.

Sudden low moaning caught Bindu's attention. The sound was of a female & it was coming from inside of the Operation Theater.

Bindu went over to the OT door & tried to peep in to check.

She was stunned with what she saw inside. Munni lay on the bed with her clothes scattered all over. Doctor saab was on top of her. Both the bodies moved in tandem.

Bindu was grown up to understand what was going on but still froze at the sight. She didn't know how to react.

Was Munni in danger?

Well, it did not seem that Munni was being forced into the act. She did not repel or make any noise. She was completely into it.

Doctor saab was feasting on her & Munni responded to his every touch & move.

This was one secret Munni had not told her.

She had surely become a woman.

Bindu was only further upset by this. She decided not to confront them. She quietly stepped back and headed home.

We're poor Bindu, her father began. Its important for you to settle down. You have siblings also & I'm getting old. I understand that you want to study. At times I hope I could help you do that but you know our situation. I will let you complete your 12th exams but then you have to promise me that you will agree to the marriage proposal like my good daughter as soon as the exams get over.

Bindu was listening to her father's words with tears in her eyes. She was happy for the fact that her father had spoken to her in so many years. She was happy that her father knew what she wanted from her life. She could acknowledge their current financial & societal position. She could also appreciate her father's view.

But she did not want to succumb to this emotional blackmail. Atleast not without a fight.

Papa, I will take up a job somewhere after my school exams. I will not be a financial burden on you. In fact, I will help you better things for our-selves. I will join a distance learning college & continue with my studies. Once I will become a teacher, all our problems will be solved.

Please give me 4 more years.

Bindu's father was listening attentively. He had this sudden respect for his daughter. His eyes were wet too. He wanted to do something for her but 4 years was not something that the society would let him agree to.

Beta, let me think about it & try and do as much as I can. I can't promise you much but I want your assurance that you will agree to whatever I decide.

Bindu was whelmed with emotions & the surprise support that she had got from her father.

She was not going to allow her-self to be over-whelmed. She had to keep her guard up. She was not at all prepared to get married.

Bindu lay down on her cot. She was staring at the stars. So much had happened so fast in her life. What she saw at the hospital today just did not leave her mind.

How could Munni do such a thing? Was she doing it for money or was she in love with that old doctor? Bindu wanted answers. She decided to confront Munni on this tomoro morning at the pond.

Bindu was sitting on the last step of the pond. Her legs dipped in the cool water. She was deep in her contemplative mode. Her mind was trying to make sense of so much that had happened in the last few days. She was lost in her bewilderment when she felt a tight squeeze from behind.

It was Munni.

She was late today. Munnis's hand carefully caressed Bindu's fragile structure. Bindu sat still with her head now buried in Munni's bosoms. Munni gave her a playful massage on her shoulders & head.

This hug was much needed, thought Bindu. She enjoyed these precious private moments with Munni.

For a moment she forgot she was angry. Regaining her senses Bindu began.

What is going on Munni? Is there something that you are not telling me? Bindu shot point blank in an instant.

Munni was startled by the sudden & direct question.

Why? What happened? Why are you saying this? Munni could only submit this in her defense.

She further hugged Bindu tightly, sensing something was not right.

Hope you are Ok Bindu. Come lets go into the pond, suggested Munni, trying to change the topic.

No, I'm not OK Munni. I want to talk today, snapped Bindu. I want to talk now.

Bindu was staring over the pond, looking for an answer. There were tears in her eyes.

Munni stared at her & Bindu's reflection in the pond. She was taken aback by Bindu's sudden assault.

I came to meet you at the hospital yesterday Munni.

Munni's heart suddenly missed a beat. Her hands lost grip of Bindu.

She wanted to run away but she was numb below her waist. Her head came down in a flash.

That old doctor was all over you Munni. Do you realize what you were doing? Did that buffoon drug you or something? For god sake please open your mouth & talk. I want to know what's happening.

Bindu was furious, sad, upset, concerned & worried.

Munni was still quiet & kept staring down.

I'm going to complain to the cops, suggested Bindu. I'm sure that doctor drugged you into this. Taking Munni's hand in her own she squeezed them re-assuringly.

You don't need worry my love. Its ok if you don't want to talk about it. I can understand. You will be just fine. I'm going to get you out of this.

Bindu had forgotten about her marriage proposal. She held Munni's hands & got up to leave.

Munni was now in tears. She burst out crying. Bindu took her in arms & consoled her. She was now genuinely concerned for Munni.

I was not drugged Bindu, whimpered Munni.

I just didn't have the courage to tell you Bindu. I was not sure how would you react. I didn't want to lose you.

I didn't know how to handle things. My family needed money & Virju introduced me to Doctor saab. I just got into this. Now its become a habit & an easy source of income.

I'm sorry Bindu, I should have told you about this. Please forgive me dear.

Munni, presented her part of the story after gathering some gumption.

Virju? Screamed Bindu. Now she was more worried about Munni's equation with Virju.

Virju was an 'enemy'. Was Munni on his side?

Tell me everything Munni. Who all are involved & since when are you doing this? I want to know every single detail & I want it now, demanded Bindu.

Munni confessed to everything one by one.

How could you Munni? Just for money & some quick favors.

You have slept with Virju, Doctor Saab, Principal Sir.

You know what are such girls called? Promise me, you will not do this anymore.

Bindu looked Munni in her eyes not wanting to believe her ears.

Promise me now, she yelled.

Please don't get mad at me Bindu. Munni was now pleading. I was going to talk to you about all this.

See in just 6 months time all my financial & educational worries are sorted. I could also convince Doctor saab to give you a job at the hospital.

Munni, was helplessly, trying to put forth a line of logic.

Bindu's mind was shut & shocked. She didn't want to talk to Munni anymore.

Munni, my parents are arranging my marriage. I don't want to get married. I want to complete my studies & take up a respectable job.

Bindu decided to tell her agony finally before leaving. Bindu got up & started to leave.

Please don't go Bindu. We need to talk. What marriage? You cant get married at this age. Tell me what happened. I will fix up everything. Munni was worried.

Bindu was a part of her life. She had always been protective about her. Life in the village had its challenges. The challenges become battles if you were poor. Munni knew what marriage at this age meant. Her mis-adventures had matured her to levels much beyond her age. Bindu's life would become a living hell. She was determined to not let this happen.

I will not let this marriage happen, Bindu.

I am going to get you out of this Munni.

Both the girls broke into an eternal tight hug. Weeping profusely.

Bindu knew Munni would stop her marriage but how was she going to get Munni out of this. She had no clue.

Munni was not sure if she actually wanted to stop doing what she was doing.

Though initially she had some reservations but now it was a part of her life. It was how her life was. But she chose not to contradict Bindu. She was relieved of the fact that Bindu had forgiven her.

Both the girls wiped off each other's tears & promised to never hide anything in the future.

Why are you late Bindu? Asked her father a little concerned.

Bindu didn't answer & crashed on her cot. She was tired & fell asleep soon.

Before Bindu could go to school, her father announced that he was going to the neighboring village to discuss a few important things regarding Bindu's marriage. He will be back by the evening.

But Father, you told me that you will re-consider this marriage proposal.

He smiled at Bindu. Bindu smiled back.

She was sure her father was going to call off the wedding & give her a new lease of life.

Bindu you have to come with me right now. You are not going to believe what I've found out.

Munni grabbed Bindu's hand & literally dragged her from the classroom to a more serene & quiet place.

Munni had used her network to find out everything wrt Bindu's marriage.

Rs 500,000. Five Lakh Bindu. That's the price your father has asked from your prospective 'groom' for your hand. He is not marrying you. He is selling you off in the name of marriage.

Bindu could feel the lump in her throat. She did not want to believe what Munni was telling her.

But Munni, he told me that he will try & let me complete my studies.....all rubbish, barged in Munni. I know all these men. They cant handle their daughters & then will have the guts to sell them off.

What shall I do now Munni? Bindu was looking at Munni like a helpless goat.

Her entire world had come crashing down.

Virju can help us. His father can tell your father to cancel the wedding. Your father will have to agree as he is the panchayat.

This will give you some time.Munni suggested.

But why will Virju help us? I mean, help me? questioned Bindu.

Bindu, he will. Trust me. Munni said assuringly with a wink.

Bindu's father had come back & announced that the marriage will happen as per the agreed plan & that he could do nothing to postpone it.

Bindu had seen him slip a package secretly to her mother. The 'advance' payment perhaps, thought Bindu.

5lakh was a big amount. It would have meant an end to all sufferings of the family. By just sacrificing one daughter, his father would get a good life for everyone.

Bindu was not in any mood to be that sacrificial goat.

I will not marry. Bindu said sternly & left.

Bindu was in a fix. She didn't want to become someone's sex slave for the rest of her life. Nor did she want to live in this hut of her parents anymore. She had lost all love & respect for them.

Though she did not appreciate what Munni did but nonetheless, she had come to respect her independence. Dignity!

She decided to break free from this clutter.

Bindu met Munni at the pond as per their regular ritual. She had gone a little earlier today as requested by Munni.

Both the girls quickly undressed & wrapped themselves in a cotton sheet & entered the pond as they did every day.

So what's the plan Munni, asked Bindu.

Munni smiled back at Bindu cunningly.

You don't have to worry about anything now Bindu. Nothing is going to happen to you.

Both the girls were waist deep into the water. Munni's full grown & developed bosoms were responding nervously to the morning cool breeze.

Bindu clung tight to her sheet. Her body was numb with cold. She could faintly feel Munni's hands on her hips. The feeling soon warmed up her frozen body. She felt sensations run across her body as if she was struck by lightning. She had not been touched like this before.

Bindu hugged Munni as tight as she could. Munni held Bindu with all her might.

Both the girls smiled in silence!

Speak to the Author Directly & Tell us how you liked SHOTS!

- **Website:** www.atmoz.in/shots
- **Email:** shots@atmoz.in
- **FB:** https://www.facebook.com/nand.agarwal.5
- **Insta:** https://www.instagram.com/nandk.agarwal/
- **Linkedin:** https://www.linkedin.com/in/nand-k-agarwal
- **Youtube:** https://www.youtube.com/channel/UCn6emTFYfCYkGMrBTW6NFGQ

Upcoming Projects:

1. **Pegs-** Each of these 8 Shots will come out as full length novels (Peg). There is a prequel & sequel to every character. Pegs will take you deeper into the world of each women character portrayed in this book. So if Shots gave you a "High", Pegs will leave you 'Sloshed". Get ready!

2. **Chirps-** Shots was written to excite...Chirps will ignite! It will compel you to look at things differently. Chirps is a contrarian take on topics that concern us daily.
    a. Democracy
    b. Votes
    c. Start up
    d. Jobs
    e. Appeasement
    f. Religion
    g. Management
    h. Profitability
    i. Life lessons
    j. Relationships & More..

3. **Vedas Simplified:** The project is untitled & in Research mode. We are making an attempt to dive deep into our rich history & come out with facts & theories for you to read & enjoy.

4. **Educational Series for Kids:** The project is untitled & in Research mode. I very strongly feel that what kids are taught in school is not good enough. Imagine my daughter is learning the same thing I learnt when I was her age! Something is wrong with this. We are making an attempt to provide a solution here.

Lucky Draw:

This being my 1st book, I humbly invite every reader to send us a feedback along with their photo with the book. My companies (Atmoz Appliances, Atmoz HR Technology, Contrarian Ventures LLP) will be very happy to encourage you.

Gifts in excess of INR 7lakhs to be won!!

- 10 M2 Atmoz Air Purifies worth INR 29990 each
- 15 M1 Atmoz Air Purifiers worth INR 19990 each
- Multiple other gifts like Atmoz Copper Bottles, Iron, Chimneys, Cook-tops & a lot more.

You may scan the code for details or visit the author page: www.atmoz.in/shots

Signing Off:

Say no to Plastic

Plant trees

Grow fruits & vegetables

Don't litter

Don't engage in road rage

Spend time with your friends & family

Have a good life!

Padhte raho!

Some Encouraging comments by my well wishers:

1. Nand- are you serious?
2. Hain!! No way
3. Chap tou jaegi…Padhega kaun?
4. Itna ideas aata kidhar se hai
5. Sach mein tune likhi hai..
6. Achchi lag rahi hai..
7. Yaar its too good!!
8. Wow..kya kahani likhi hai
9. Man..its so freakingly gripping
10. End kitni jaldi ho jaati hai…give me more!
11. Nand and romance- kya baat hai!!
12. Make a web series out of it- Must read ☺
13. Get one today-I'm serious!

www.ingramcontent.com/pod-product-compliance
Ingram Content Group UK Ltd.
Pitfield, Milton Keynes, MK11 3LW, UK
UKHW041843200726
13854UKWH00005BA/2037